PUPPY LOVE

DOGG PACK SERIES

EVIE MITCHELL

THUNDER THIGHS PUBLISHING

Editor: Nicole Wilson, Evermore Editing
http://www.evermoreediting.wixsite.com/info

ACKNOWLEDGEMENT OF COUNTRY

I acknowledge the Traditional Custodians of the lands on which I write, the Ngunnawal people, and pay my respect to elders both past and present.

I acknowledge the continued and deep spiritual relationship of the Australian Aboriginal and Torres Strait Islander peoples' to this land, and their unique cultural and spiritual relationships to the land, waters and seas and their rich contribution to society.

Always was, always will be.

To Hendrix, the greatest dog that ever lived.

Little man, you were our heart, and we are lost
without you.

Thanks for being a herald, a rescuer, a protector,
a squeaky destroyer, a wonderful big brother, our
joy, and the most amazing loving pupper in the
universe.

We miss you, buddy.
Daddy and I love you forever.

PUPPY LOVE

Kat

Hayden Dogg is frustrating. Annoying. Arrogant.

And way too caring for his own good.

I said yes to the charity calendar, expecting to cuddle cute animals-- not get an eyeful of his rather impressive chest.

We might fight like cats and dogs but maybe, deep down, there's room for a little puppy love.

Warning: This book is filled with delicious tension, cute puppies, and a ride like no other. Get thee a hot guy, and maybe a fun rabbit, and settle in. You're in for a delicious treat!

CHAPTER 1

"That's it, work it, baby. Uh-huh, you got it. Give me a little more sass. That's it. Shake that tail like your mommy showed you."

I snapped pictures, changing the angle, attempting to snap just the right picture.

Lulu glanced over her shoulder, offering me a coy look.

"That's the money shot!" I yelled, dropping my phone and reaching over to pat her head. "Who's a good girl? Are you my good girl? Would you like a treat, my little good girl?"

The silky terrier lost her mind at the word treat, her tail wagging frantically as she tap-danced on the platform.

"Here you go, my good girl." I fed her a liver treat from my pocket, flicking through the photos while she crunched.

Ah, fuck.

A photographer I was *not*. The images were blurry, poorly lit, and angled wrong. Instead of looking adorable, Lulu looked like some kind of hellhound with glowing eyes and bared teeth. Even her cute little smile appeared like a snarl.

"Ah shit. Lulu, I'm sorry, I can't use any of these."

The silky snuffled at my pocket, searching for more treats.

"Here you go, you little hussy." I fed her another treat, flicking back through the shots I'd taken. One seemed like it could be okay if I superimposed some normal eyes over her glowing ones.

DR.DOGG

Dogg Fam! What do you think of this picture?

I sent the glowing eyes to my family chat.

J-WOOD

WTF is that? Some kind of devil spawn?

ASH

Dude. That dog needs to be put down, not adopted.

MADOGG

I'm not saying I wouldn't adopt,
but you'd have to convince me
that it wasn't riddled with rabies.

DADDYDOGG

I rate it as a 0.5/5 for photo
skills. Hope you're a better vet
than photographer.

RYAN

Dude... *thumbs down emoji*

SAMTHEPUP

Does it have superpowers? Can
we get a dog, Dad?

DADDYDOGG

Absolutely not!

MADOGG

We'll discuss it tonight.

DADDYDOGG

Like hell we will! Isn't a new
baby enough?

MADOGG

You'd deprive your youngest
son of a dog because we just
had a baby?

DADDYDOGG

I'm not depriving him of
anything!

MADOGG

Except a dog.

DADDYDOGG

Karrie, we'll talk about this later.

JAMES

Huh-oh! I'm guessing this
means what I think it means…

J-WOOD

Can I come for dinner? Cause
this shit is hilarious!

SAMTHEPUP

Does this mean we're getting
a dog?

ASH

Looks like it, kiddo!

RYAN

Uh-oh…

SAMTHEPUP

:) :) :) !!!

I sighed, dropping the phone to pinch the
bridge of my nose.

My family was a wild pack—and I meant
that in the nicest way possible. Dad had
married Karen last year, and they'd just had
their first baby—Janeane—last month. Of my
six siblings, Janeane was the only one related to

me by blood. The rest—Jay, James, Ash, Ryan and Sam were adopted or foster kids that Dad had taken in over the years. Only Ash, at eighteen, Ryan, at fourteen, and Sam, at nine, were still at home. Jay and James were all in their twenties and either working in Capricorn Cove or at college studying.

It was times like this that I both missed living at home and felt supremely relieved to have at least a few miles between us.

I looked back at the picture of Lulu, frustrated as all hell by my lack of photographic ability.

The plan had been two-fold. First, we were gonna use the images I took to create a charity calendar and raise money for our new rescue shelter. We were also going to start placing ads on our social media and website.

When I'd taken over the animal practice from my former mentor, I'd decided to add a rescue shelter to the back of the property. The shelter had only been operational for a few months, but already we were nearing capacity, and I wanted my charges to find good homes— not stay in a temporary facility forever.

"Sorry, Lulu. I guess we're shit outta luck."

"Out of luck?" June, my receptionist, poked her head around the doorway. "What's up, Doc?"

A child of the British punk era, June had never outgrown wild-coloured hair, leather jackets, piercings, or her love for punk.

I held up my phone, sighing as she tutted over the pictures. I didn't know if it was the Brit in her, but June had a tut that always made me think of a proper school principal expressing disappointment in her ward.

You really need to get out more.

"You know, my niece and nephew are visiting next week. They'll be staying for three months before Henry heads off on his fellowship at that college—gosh, what's its name? The one with the giant oak trees."

I hid a smile. "Ravenburn? As in the only college in our town?"

"That's the one!" June slapped a hand on the table, startling Lulu. "Sorry, precious. Come here, let me hold you close."

"So, Henry is a photographer as well?" I asked, attempting to steer the conversation back to our current predicament.

"Absolutely not. The boy is completely illiterate when it comes to anything art. Except for books—obviously."

"Obviously," I agreed.

Henry, as June had repeatedly bragged, held a doctorate in modern literature. He lectured at King's College on gendered writing and had forty-three books to his name—all of which were bestsellers, even the non-fiction ones.

"No, it's Kat who is the artist in the family. A wild heart, that one. Takes after me, I suppose. Her mother—my sister—never did roam far from Burford."

"Kat's a photographer?" I asked, desperate to get to the point of this conversation.

"Oh, my yes," June said, her fingers finding Lulu's perfect spot. The little dog leaned into her, a muffled huff of contentment escaping her. "And I'm sure she'd be more than happy to assist."

I looked back down at the phone that lay on the table between us—Lulu's demonic image staring up at me.

"I'd seriously appreciate any help I can get."

June pressed a kiss to Lulu's head. "Don't you worry, darling. You leave it all to me."

CHAPTER 2

Kat

I threw the door open with a groan, kicking my feet out and heaving myself out of the car.

"Never again," I declared, pressing my hands to my lower back as I attempted to stretch out the knots. "Honestly, Henry. What were we thinking?"

"It wasn't that bad," my brother said with a grin, flicking his dark hair out of his eyes. "We only nearly died three times."

"Three is three too many."

"Well, tell these Astipians to drive on the right side of the road."

I snorted. "They drive on the same side as us!"

"You're here!"

We both turned towards the ramshackle old beach cottage, grinning as Auntie June leapt off the top stair, bounding across the grass to throw herself at us. "My babies!" She laughed, squeezing us both tight to her.

We hadn't seen our aunt in over three years. Not since she'd last returned to England for a visit that had involved far too much alcohol, laughter, and eating.

To say she was my favourite relative was an understatement. June was the person I most aspired to be in this world.

"Come inside, let's get you a bracing cup of tea and some biscuits. I want to hear everything!"

We trailed her like ducklings, following her into the bright and airy cottage.

The interior resembled a rock hall of fame more than anything. Mementos from June's days of trailing bands around the world hung on every wall. There were signed posters and photos, a collage of guitar picks, and even a signed guitar. Our aunt had been a roadie, a personal assistant, and a groupie at various points in her life. Rumour had it that at least four famous songs had been written as odes to her.

Then she'd fallen in love with an Astipian

guitarist and moved to the island Kingdom to be with him. They'd never married but loved each other with a fierce passion that continued to this day.

"And where is Uncle Don?" Henry asked, looking around the place.

"Out back checking on the smoker. He's determined to give you a proper Astipian welcome, the silly man."

My mouth began to water, my stomach grumbling at the thought of smoked ribs and Uncle Don's delicious cornbread.

"It's been far too long since we had some of Don's cooking."

June pulled me into her side, giving me another tight squeeze. "Yes, it has. Oh, how I've missed you. Come, let's pop you out on the deck and get some tea into you."

"Tea sounds wonderful."

We settled in the sunshine, the sounds of the waves and the call of sea birds a gentle background to our excited chatter.

"You're losing your accent," I teased my aunt over a cup of perfectly brewed tea.

"Never!" she gasped, laying a bejewelled hand on her ample bosom. "Hush your mouth!"

Henry and I laughed, accepting a refill of tea from Don.

"Now, tell us about this fellowship, young

man," Don ordered, settling back in his seat. "Ravenburn is a prestigious school."

Henry nodded, his teacup sliding into the saucer with a satisfying click. "I'm still not sure how I managed to wrangle it, but the school is happy to have me, and I'm thrilled to have the opportunity to be funded to finish my research."

"What Henry is trying to say is that he can't wait to spend time in some boring library surrounded by musty books and positively frothing as he reads sonnets or some such nonsense." I rolled my eyes. "Give me sun and sand any day."

Don and June chuckled as Henry ignored me.

"We'll be in the country for around twelve months. Spending the summer with you, then six at the College and another three travelling after. I'm quite looking forward to my first summer in Astipia."

"And what will you be doing while your brother is studying?" June asked, reaching for a shortbread biscuit.

"I'm looking to freelance while here. Hopefully get out to some of the national parks and capture some photos. My agent back home wants to do a gallery showing in November. I suspect I'll have enough images for her to pull something together between now and then."

June considered me over the edge of her teacup. I glanced away, faking interest in the biscuits.

"Sounds like you'll both be keeping busy," Don said, pushing up. "Just remember to make time to enjoy life. And on that note, let me just go check on these ribs. They should be about ready."

I watched Don walk off, enjoying the sun on my face and the gentle breeze as it teased my hair.

"I can see why you love this town," I commented to June as I tilted my head back. "This spot in particular."

"Speaking of this town." June leaned in, reaching over to place a hand on my knee. "Would you have some time in your busy doing nothing calendar to help me out with a project? I'm woefully out of my depth, I'm afraid."

"Of course. What do you need?"

"We're attempting to do a calendar for the shelter. We need the images by the end of the month so they can be formatted and ready for the printers. We're wanting to sell them starting in October. But the photos are terrible. I'm afraid Dr. Dogg—"

"Wait, your boss's name is Dog?"

She chuckled. "Yes, the poor man. Double-G though. Anyway, the poor poppet is rather out of his depth technology-wise. The photographs he takes are... well, best deleted, and his camera burned, if I'm honest."

I laughed.

"Would you mind terribly if—"

"Of course not." I grinned. "Anything for my favourite aunt."

June squeezed my knee, leaning back in her seat. "And this is why you're my favourite."

"Hey!" Henry protested. "I thought I was the favourite."

"You failed to dedicate your last book to me. You've been quite dead to me for months, dear."

CHAPTER 3

Kat

Perhaps I'd be more amused by the teasing from my family if it weren't for the onslaught of dick pictures, I'd found on my phone this morning.

"Read another!" Don demanded, tears streaming down his laughing face. "These are classic!"

It appeared that Capricorn Cove had something of a woman drought. And unfortunately for me, I'd left a dating app signed in on my phone. I'd tried dating after Gavin had dumped me six months ago and immediately taken up with his secretary. After three disastrous dates—including one where the man had told me he wished to knock me up in order to spread his seed across the world but didn't want to be a father—I'd abandoned any thoughts of romance and left the platform.

Unfortunately, I'd forgotten to uninstall it. The app had updated my location overnight, and I'd woken to two hundred and thirty-four messages from the woman-hungry men of this town.

"Oh!" Henry began to snicker, his shoulders shaking as he scrolled through my phone. "Listen to this one. 'What movie title would describe your dating life? I'll go first—Free Willy.'"

The table lost it, June, Don, and Henry all roaring with laughter as I tried gallantly to summon a modicum of amusement at my current predicament.

If I wasn't so jet-lagged, perhaps I'd feel less stabby.

Most of the messages had been okay. A few had even been rather lovely, and if I'd been interested, I might have even allowed them to take me out for a cup of coffee. But the unsolicited dick pics that had assaulted my sandpaper-like eyes had left me in a foul mood.

I rubbed them, frustrated by the jetlag and overall exhaustion.

Whoever thought sending a picture of their

*pickle—particularly while sitting on a toilet—
was the way to a woman's heart?*

June, of course, found it hilarious.

"Oh! Give it here. I know just what to reply."

She typed in a reply as Henry and Don read over her shoulder, both of them exploding into gales of laughter as she hit send.

June turned the phone, holding it out for me to read.

> Alexander and the Terrible, Horrible, No Good, Very Bad Day.

Very apt, June.

I lifted my teacup in a weak acknowledgment of her brilliance.

"Don, is this Edward?"

Don took the offered phone, squinting at the picture.

"The wrist tattoo is right," he agreed, shaking his head. "It's barely nine in the morning. What kind of man sends a dick pic at this time of day? At least wine and dine a woman first."

June screenshotted the message. "I'm sending this to his mother. Susan did not raise that boy to be flashing his penis about the place."

I dropped my head into my hand, groaning as June and Don began to pour over my phone, attempting to identify the multiple dick-sending perps.

It is far too early, and I am far too under-caffeinated for these shenanigans.

"I'm gonna go for a walk. Is there a café nearby? I think I need some fresh air and a strong shot to get me through today."

June nodded, her head still bent over my phone. "Down the end of the street, turn left, and follow the esplanade until you reach town. Look for the Bronze Horseman."

"Got it." I pushed up from my seat, Henry following.

"What? You're not staying to read more of the 'Kat dating chronicles'?" I asked, more than a little pissy with my brother.

He reached out, ruffling my hair. "I know you're just jet-lagged. I'm only coming to make sure you don't fall asleep at the café and get kidnapped by one of these desperate and dateless men."

"None of them would kidnap you," June said, her fingers flying over my phone screen. "Except perhaps Matthew. But he's rarely allowed out since he got the ankle monitor."

"That fills me with such confidence," I drawled dryly. "We'll be back in a few."

"Have fun."

Outside, the sun warmed my skin as seagulls called greetings in the distance.

"This town is a strange mixture of quaint and kitsch," Henry remarked, as we walked.

"You're considering how to use it in a future novel, aren't you?"

My brother shot me a grin. "Have to earn back the title of favourite somehow."

I shoved him, laughing. "No chance."

A woman glanced our way, hand in hand with the man beside her. For a moment, her gaze lingered on my brother before her partner caught sight of her direction and called her attention back to him. She laughed as he growled something, the words lost in the space between us, but his intention was clear as he leaned down, capturing her face in one hand and kissing her possessively.

My heart gave a little tug, a sigh slipping free before I could catch it.

Dick pics, Kat. Remember? Dating is a waste of time.

"What?"

I looked up at Henry, considering him with an objective eye. Lean but muscular, slightly above average height with a kind of Harry Potter-esque look about him, my brother had his fair share of love interests. Unfortunately for them, his love remained centred in the pages of books.

"Nothing," I muttered, shaking off my morose thoughts. "Look, there's the Bronze Horseman. Let's hope they do decent coffee."

As we waited to cross the road, a car turned, driving down the street just as a cat ran out from an alley, darting across the street.

"Wait!"

"Stop!"

The car's tires locked, a screeching sound piercing the air as the driver hit the brakes. A woman in baggy overalls jumped out, her face pale.

"Shit, did I hit him this time?"

This time?

Henry and I ran over, crouching down beside the prone cat.

"I didn't see," I said, reaching out a hand.

"Should you touch it?" Henry asked. "What if it—"

"Excuse me," interrupted a smooth voice. A hand settled on my shoulder, gently brushing me to the side. "I got this."

A man crouched beside me, immediately taking over the situation. He glanced my way, offering me a cocky smirk as he turned to the driver, completely dismissing me.

"Alright. What's happened, Annie?"

The woman in overalls shuffled anxiously from foot to foot, her hands clenching and unclenching. "I think I finally hit him. Maybe. I'm not sure. I think... shit!"

He reached for the cat.

"Wait," I said, adrenaline pumping through my veins. "I don't think you should touch him. What if he has rabies or something?"

The guy ignored my warning, pressing a hand to the cat's pulse point. The cat opened its eyes, giving a soft growl.

"Oh, hush," the guy told the cat sternly. "There's not even blood."

My eyebrows flew up, outraged at his complete dismissal of this poor creature's suffering. "I'm sorry, did you just—"

The guy reached for the cat's face, peeling back his lips and checking its gum. "Give me a second, I'll be right with you, Ma'am."

Ma'am!? Of all the rude, self-centred—who does this guy think he is?

"Alright, the cat is fine." The guy rocked back on his heels. "Looks like he's just faking, folks."

"Faking?" I repeated, staring down at the floppy cat who was obviously dying. "Bollocks, he's faking. Look at him! He's practically comatose! We need to get him to a vet. We need—"

The cat, perhaps recognising that he wasn't getting any further sympathy, sprang from his prone position, back arching to hiss at the man.

"Now, Gus," the guy said with a waggle of his finger. "We've talked about this."

The cat took a swipe at the guy, then darted between the driver's legs, disappearing back the way he'd come.

Well. I mean... well.

The man beside me twisted, holding out a hand. "I'm Hayden. You must be new in town."

I took his offered hand, then immediately dropped it, remembering my anger at the man.

"Sorry, what right do you have to come barging into this scene and declare that—"

"I'm Henry." My brother held out his hand. "This is Kat, ignore her, she's jet-lagged and not normally this ragey. Yes, we're new in town."

"I'm not ragey," I protested, glaring at my traitor of a sibling. "I'm put out by this man's overbearing, know-it-all attitude. Who is he to come in here and just take over like—"

"Excuse me," the driver interrupted my tirade. "Sorry to break up this meet-cute but if all is well then I really need to get to work. Could you guys maybe...." She made shooing motions with her hands.

"No worries, Annie," Hayden said, looking at the woman. "I should be going as well."

He stood, shooting me another grin. "It was nice to meet you, Kat. And you, Henry. Hope you enjoy your stay. Maybe we could—"

I grimaced, expecting him to ask me out.

"—meet again under less dramatic circumstances." With that, the man had the gall to just walk off as if nothing had happened.

"Where does he think—"

My brother pulled me to a stand, his hand firm on my back as he turned us, pressing me towards the restaurant.

"Caffeine will make you feel better. And, if we're lucky, they may have some pastry options to add some sugar to the bitterness you're spewing." He paused for a second, his head tilting to one side. "That's not a bad line. I should write that down."

While he pulled his phone out to add the note, I twisted, looking over my shoulder at the disappearing douchebag.

Well, at least today can't get any worse.

CHAPTER 4

Hayden

"Do we know anyone who would be able to draw up a paternity arrangement?" Julie, my colleague, asked.

I looked up from the piglet I was examining. "Excuse me? Julie, is there something I should know?"

She laughed, shaking her head. "Not for me. One of our new clients, Mae. Her bitch, Tutu, was knocked up by the rescue next door. She wants to draw up a puppy paternity arrangement."

I blinked. "Well, that's new. The only person I can think of is Roger. And even then, I don't think he does dog-related agreements."

Julie nodded. "How's Mr. Piggie?"

I flipped the piglet over, ignoring his squealed protests and kicking limbs.

"Better. The wound is nearly healed. Another week and it'll be like it never happened."

"Should we clear him for adoption? We've had a few expressions of interest—including from the local petting zoo."

I righted the piglet, grinning as he took off, running back to the far end of his enclosure, and dived headfirst into his feed.

"Yes, I think it's time. Get June to screen the applicants, but hopefully, we'll have him settled in the next two weeks and can free up some room for our next visitor."

Julie tilted her head to one side, amusement dancing in her eyes. "And the vizsla cross dachshund puppy?"

I glanced over at where the puppy sat watching me. As soon as I looked his way, his tail started wagging, his body whipping back and forth with the movement.

"Not yet," I said, knowing I was delaying the inevitable. "He's still too little."

Julie grinned. "Uh-huh. Sure."

I narrowed my eyes at her. "Don't give me that. Don't give me that judgment."

She chuckled. "Why don't you just admit you're smitten and adopt him?"

I glanced at the adorable puppy with his red colouring, white chest, and floppy ears, he was bound to get snatched up by a family.

"Because." The excuses all died on my tongue, my heart giving a little pinch at the thought of him being owned by anyone else.

"Because?" she prompted.

June saved me from answering.

"Hello, Doc! And Julie. You're both about to fall in love with me all over again."

I pushed up to a stand, desperately trying to avoid looking at the puppy who was watching me—his tail whipping once more.

"Again? I don't remember falling in love the first time."

"That's because before you realise how much you need me, I'm already deep in your heart." June stuck her fingers into the puppy's enclosure, grinning when he frantically lapped at them. "Has he given in and adopted this one yet?"

"Not yet," Julie confirmed with a laugh. "But he's coming around."

"I can't adopt a dog," I protested, even though my heart ached at the thought of this pup going to someone else.

"Well, Hendrix here—"

"Hendrix?"

June nodded firmly. "Little Hendrix. Named for the great man himself. Hendrix is a rock star, and I foresee nothing but awesomeness in this little man's future."

I'd avoided naming the puppy for this exact reason. Looking at his adorable little face, his eyes bright with love and devotion, I finally gave in. "Alright. Bring him out. Julie, can you take care of the paperwork for Hendrix?"

The two women slapped palms, both of them laughing.

"Knew it! He was always going to give in."

"And a day earlier than Don predicted. He owes me a latte."

I rolled my eyes at both of them. "Can we get to work, please?"

Julie handed me little Hendrix, the puppy immediately scrambling up my chest to lap energetically at my face, his paws far too big for his tiny body.

"Hello, little man," I cooed. "Are you my little buddy? My little Hendrix?"

Hendrix's tail wagged frantically, and then I felt it—excitement pee.

With a sigh, I held him out, looking down at my shirt.

"Oh, he is totally your dog," Julie giggled. "He's even marked you now."

I made a face, holding him out to her. "Can you hold him for a minute? I'll just take this off. I have a spare in the office."

She took the puppy, offering him praise as I whipped my shirt off, then handed Hendrix back to me.

"Now, why should I love you, June?"

She eyed my chest, her eyebrows raising as she called, "Kat? Can you come in here, please?"

Kat? As in...?

Around the corner of the shelter stepped a long, pale, perfectly shaped leg. It was followed by another, which was attached to ample hips, a curvy torso, generous breasts, delightfully sculpted shoulders, a delicious neck, and a face that would make angels weep.

Hendrix let out a sigh.

Oh, buddy, I feel you.

My cock—not normally one for spontaneous demonstrative reactions— immediately hardened.

It's the busty brunette from this morning.

Images assaulted me—the two of us tangled in sheets, my mouth worshipping her body, her riding me to a lusty, satisfying climax.

I want to taste her.

The thought was so startling, so absolutely

out of character, that I nearly dropped Hendrix.

"Hayden, this is my niece, Kat. Kat, meet Doctor Dogg."

Kat's grin froze on her face, her eyebrows lifting. "Wait, *this* is the tech-challenged vet?"

"Guilty." I juggled my puppy, holding out a hand for her to shake. "It's good to see you again, Kat."

She automatically took my offered hand, my cock jumping as something sparked between us.

"You two know each other?" June asked, her eyebrow cocked in question.

"Gus did his dash-and-die stunt," I explained. "He's fine."

"I thought you'd be older," Kat said, her tone accusatory as she glared at me.

"Uh... okay? I mean, I guess I could try and add a few years right now." I closed my eyes, pretending to concentrate. "Did it work?"

June and Julie giggled as Kat gave me a bland stare.

He swings, and he misses folks. Pull it together, Dogg. You got this.

"Do you always greet your guests without a shirt?" Kat asked, her accent crisp as she stared pointedly at my naked chest.

"Only the lucky ones."

Kat's lips pressed into a thin line, her eyebrows curving down into two disapproving slashes.

Uh-oh. She really doesn't like me.

I decided to change the subject. "June mentioned that you might be available to take some pictures for us." I held little Hendrix up. "This guy is volunteering to be the cover model."

"Did you reconsider my idea about the nude calendar?" June asked, reaching over to scratch Hendrix behind the ear. "I'd be more than happy to sell them to the ladies at bowling."

Heat began to creep up my neck.

"Ah, no. We're not doing that. Just animals will be fine."

June sighed noisily. "Well, if you change your mind...."

"I'll let you know."

I glanced at Kat, expecting to find her looking amused, instead, she appeared downright annoyed. Unsurprisingly, this did nothing to relieve the SCUD missile in my pants.

Dude, you're so in the Dogg house.

CHAPTER 5

Kat

What, I wondered, *have I done in a past life to deserve this?*

"As much as I hope you ladies like what you see"—the odious man ran a hand down his chest with a laugh—"I'm just gonna go get another shirt. I'll be right back."

With the puppy still in his arms, he headed down the aisle, calling greetings to the various animal residents currently living in the shelter.

June turned to me with a bright smile.

"Well, it's not every day you get an eyeful of your future husband right off the bat."

I raised my eyebrow. "Excuse me?"

She waved a hand. "It was just a dream I

had about you two last night. FYI, you made a beautiful bride."

I gave my aunt a disgruntled side-eye. "Don't start matchmaking. It's not going to happen. I'm here for a good time, not a long time."

She raised her hands in a 'who me' gesture. "I would never."

"Besides, he's not my type."

June laughed. "Darling, he's everyone's type."

I shook my head. "Nope. I don't date arrogant men who have no sense of decorum."

"Arrogant? What are you—"

"That's better." Hayden returned, the puppy trailing him, the dog's little teeth attempting to catch his jean leg. "Kat, shall we get started? I appreciate you agreeing to help out."

I shot a glare at June then slapped on my most professional expression. "Sure, let's do it."

He gestured for me to follow him as he led me down the shelter aisle, pointing out the various rescue animals and giving me a quick rundown as his puppy, Hendrix, trotted along beside him.

"This is the room I thought you could use," he said, opening up a small examination room, hitting the light switch.

"Oh, no. Definitely not. The lighting in here is going to make every animal look like some kind of Frankenstein being." I pointed at the fluorescent bulbs blinking to life above us. "Never shoot under these. Ever. Unless you're intending on doing a horror shoot."

He laughed, flicking the lights off. "Noted. Probably why every shot I took looked like an ode to *Psycho*. What would you suggest instead?"

"Do you have an outdoor space? Like a dog run or something?"

"Yeah, right this way."

He led me through a side door and outside into a large yard.

"Wow. This is next level."

Surrounded by tall fencing, the place was every animal's dream. Lots of space to run, different climbing activities, a sandpit, a water area, trees, and a heap of what looked like treat activity toys scattered around.

"Thanks. This is the play area, but we've got three yards in total, the other two are for training. Will this work, or do you want to see the others?"

I shook my head, lifting my camera to begin snapping test shots. "No, this works. We can position the animals in different locations for a bit of variety. Is it just dogs, or do you want me to shoot other animals?"

Hayden cocked a thumb at the building behind us. "All those animals need a home. Except for Claudette, but she's off to a sanctuary."

"Claudette?"

Hayden grinned. "Follow me."

He led me out to a barn, calling a greeting to the various animals inside. Staff waved as they made their rounds or examined animals, their owners hovering anxiously nearby.

"This is our big animal area. We mostly get horses and cows, pigs, and the occasional goat. But this, this Claudette."

He stopped in front of a giant stall that had an opening at the rear.

"Oh... oh wow."

The camel considered me with her big brown eyes, her tail flicking lazily at some flies.

"Claudette was rescued from an out-of-business circus. They'd offloaded the rest of the animals, but poor Claudette here couldn't find a home." He reached out, giving her a firm scratch. The camel leaned into his hand, making a huffing sound.

"She's a character," he said with a laugh. "Did you want to pat her?"

I reached out a hesitant hand, yelping

when Claudette flicked her head back, her large jaw opening in a yawn.

"She does that. It means she's happy."

I nodded, my heart pounding. "Maybe I'll just take some pictures instead."

"Suit yourself, but you're missing out. She's a little love bug."

"Or not so little. And I happen to like my fingers, thank you very much."

Hayden chuckled as Claudette nuzzled him. "She has yet to claim any fingers. Toes are a whole other story."

I lifted my camera, a reluctant smile pulling at my lips as I snapped shots of Claudette and Dr. Dogg.

"Did you need me to do anything?" he asked, feeding Claudette a sliver of apple from a Ziplock bag he'd pulled from one of his cargo pants pockets.

"Not yet. I'm just testing light and exposure. Today I'll just do a few test snaps around the place—you might like to throw them up on your social media to tease what's coming."

He nodded, once again scratching Claudette's forehead. "Sounds good. Thanks for helping out, Kat. I seriously appreciate it."

I considered him through the lens of my

camera, capturing his easy smile and the faint laugh lines around his eyes.

I hated to say it, but the man had charm in spades. Despite being an arrogant so-and-so, he seemed to genuinely care about his wards, slipping them pats and treats as we worked our way through his menagerie of creatures great and small.

I met Tony the Ostrich, the four horses of the apocalypse, Damien the giant tortoise, and a raft of chickens, dogs, and cats. There was even a small piglet running around one of the yards, June chasing it down as his owner watched on.

"How did you get into this line of work?" I asked, capturing the four horses as they sprinted from one side of the paddock to the other, kicking up their heels in play.

"Well, with a last name like Dogg, some people would say I'm born for it. But the fact is, my dad is an animal lover. Well, a lover of all things, if I'm honest. He was always bringing home strays—human and animal. I grew up surrounded by rescue creatures. It felt only right to find a way to continue that work."

I glanced at him, camera still poised to shoot. "I'm not sure I know of many vet practices that have shelters as well."

"We're a small town but tend to get more

than our fair share of strays. The pound is a kill shelter, and I just can't condone killing an animal because we can't find it a good home in a short timeframe."

I dropped the camera, considering him. "You're not what I thought," I finally admitted, loathed that these words were coming out of my mouth.

He raised an eyebrow. "No?"

I turned back to the horses, raising my camera to begin snapping off more images. "Don't let it go to your head. It doesn't mean I like you."

Yet. You don't like him yet.

I shoved the thought away, locking it in my emotional dungeon.

"Alright, I better get back to the real work," Hayden said as we circled back to the main shelter. "I have surgery this afternoon."

"Of course." I patted my camera. "I'll give June the images tonight. You guys can choose which ones you like the feel of, and that's the direction we'll go for the photo shoot."

Hayden shook his head. "To be honest, this is far more than I expected. I was thinking of a few images slapped on a calendar we could sell at the Halloween markets later this year. You're going above and beyond for me. Thanks."

I shuffled, uncomfortable with his praise.

"Think nothing of it. June is my favourite aunt. I'd do anything for her."

"Still." Hayden tucked his hands in his pockets, rocking on his heels as he considered me. "Look, Kat. I just want to clear the air a little. About this morning—"

"Hayden! We need you!" A shout came from the clinic, a woman dressed in scrubs waving frantically at him from the doorway.

"Shit, sorry. Duty calls. Thanks again!" He took off, sprinting across the yard towards the door.

I couldn't help but admire his perfect bubble butt as he moved.

Down, Kat. Remember what happened the last time you fell for a cocky foreigner?

I rubbed absently at my chest.

As if hearing my traitorous thoughts, June appeared, a sleeping Hendrix cradled in her arms.

"He's single, you know."

I shot her a droll look. "Don't start."

She grinned. "I'm just saying."

"And I'm just saying no."

She juggled the puppy, moving him into the crook of one arm and wrapping her other around my waist. "Shall we pop this little poppet down for his nap and go get some lunch? There's a lovely bar in town that does delightful sliders."

"Sounds great."

"And perhaps while we're eating, we can look through your photos. Did you get a picture of Hayden's chest, perchance?"

I hip-checked her. "June!"

"What? I'm sixty, not dead!"

CHAPTER 6

Hayden

My phone rang, interrupting the pleasant dream I'd been enjoying. It had featured a rather naked Kat allowing me to enact certain liberties upon her person.

This better be good. Things were just starting to get interesting.

I hit accept, rubbing at my dry eyes as Hendrix protested from his curled spot on the bed beside me.

Tell me about it, buddy.

"This is Hayden."

"Um, hey Hayden, it's Tim. Look, I know it's early and your day off and all, but... ah... we kind of have a unique problem at the clinic."

I rocked up to sit on the edge of my bed. "Hit me with it. Is it another rescue?"

"Ah, no. Not even close." Tim sounded nervous. "I don't know how to describe this, but...."

When he didn't say anything for a long beat, I cracked.

"Just tell me."

"June uploaded some of the photos her niece took of you and Hendrix onto our social media last night. It kind of went viral. We're being inundated with requests to adopt you. I think... I... apparently, there's a woman from the South Island looking to organise a tour bus to meet you. We've got women arriving and lining up out the door to take photos. There's even a news crew here. Our emails are going crazy. The phone is ringing off the hook asking for your number and if you're single. I... I'm not sure what to do."

I blinked, pulled the phone away from my ear, and checked the date.

"Dude, it's too late for April Fools. This isn't funny."

"Hayden, I wouldn't joke about this. There's a line around the corner. One lady is in a wedding dress!"

I scrubbed a hand over my face. "Okay, let

me just... let me just have a shower and grab some coffee. I'll be there shortly."

"A—you're gonna have a shower? A shower! THIS IS NO TIME TO LOOK PRETTY!" Tim screamed down the phone. "There are women throwing underwear at our door!"

The panic in his tone finally cut through my sleepy haze. "Fine, I'll be there shortly."

"Wear body armour," he warned. "They're gonna tear you apart."

———

I'd assumed Tim, known for his dramatics, had been exaggerating. But upon arrival, I saw that, if anything, the man had undersold the situation. The clinic was awash with women, animals, and signs that read things like, *I'm ready to do it Dogg-y style.*

For a town that had a female drought, we were suddenly in a flood of feminism. I briefly wondered if it might be worth sending out an SOS – *Men of Capricorn Cove. Women are flooding my clinic. Come find your wife!*

"Hayden!" June called a greeting as I stumbled into the chaos of the break room. "You'll be excited to learn that adoption numbers are up!"

"June." I placed Hendrix on the ground, keeping a firm hold of his lead. "What did you do?"

She beamed at me, then pointed one long finger, tipped with a blood-red nail, towards the woman currently hunched over a mug of coffee in the corner of the room. "Blame Kat. It was all her doing."

"Excuse me?" the Brit asked, lifting her head from her coffee contemplation. "My doing? How is this my fault? All I did was take a picture."

"And that picture is the one that launched a million dreams," June sighed happily. "I always knew I'd be part of a viral revolution one day."

Kat rolled her eyes.

"Alright, so we've gone viral. What does that actually *mean*?" I asked, gesturing out the doors. "Do I go and shake some hands? Maybe encourage adoption?"

"Look, unless you want to get swarmed by women asking if you're as good with pussies as you are with dogs, I'd lay low," June advised, lifting a ringing phone from the hook. "Welcome to the Dogg House Animal Clinic and Rescue, how can I direct your call today? Oh, Doctor Dogg isn't working at the moment. Can I—"

I looked away, narrowing my gaze on Kat. "And you're just going to stand there?"

She cocked one eyebrow. "I'm just here to take pictures and drink your coffee—terrible as it is. My duties start and finish here." She patted her camera.

A chant started from the reception area.

"Doctor Dogg! Doctor Dogg!"

Kat grinned, the first genuine smile I'd seen on her lips since I'd met her. "Your fan club awaits, Doctor."

I poked my tongue out at her, making a face. "You're not funny."

"On the contrary, I'm hilarious. You're just cranky you have a million stalkers trying to get a piece of your rooster."

"My—" I barked out a laugh. "Okay, that's good."

She grinned, pushing off the wall and dumping the coffee remains in the sink. "If you want this to go away, then you need a dummy."

"Huh?"

"A fake. A stand-in. Tell the good ladies of the world you're taken, but you appreciate their support for the shelter. Get someone to pass around a bucket, and see if you can't collect some charitable donations while people are interested. Milk it, Hayden, for all this is worth."

I stared at the woman before me, the cogs in my head slowly ticking over.

Fake girlfriend. That could work.

"You're right." I tossed Hendrix's lead to June, calling, "Keep him safe for me." Then I reached out, caught Kat's hand, and began to pull us both towards the reception doors.

"What are you doing?" she screeched, digging her heels in and attempting to free herself.

"Taking your advice."

I threw open the door, stepping us into reception.

The noise level reached fever pitch as I did, women shaking their signs and screaming at the top of their lungs, which sent Ingrid—our resident parrot—into her nesting box.

Sorry, Ingrid.

It took a few tries for the noise to settle.

"Welcome to the Dogg House, I'm Hayden, and this is—"

The screaming began again, a round-robin affair that echoed outside until finally, they settled once more.

"As I was saying, I'm Hayden, and this is my partner Kat." I dropped her hand, using mine to propel her forward. "Say hi, Kat."

"Hi," she repeated as the death stares of a

hundred women landed on her. "Um, welcome?"

"We're so happy to have you here today," I told them with an easy smile. "Never thought I might win Astipia's Sexiest Man."

There were sighs and chuckles as the tension in the room lightened.

"While I can't help you out with a date, I'd be more than happy to take pictures, give hugs, and tell you more about the work of the clinic and rescue if you're interested."

"Oh, honey, if you're speaking, I'm gonna be listening!" A woman yelled from the back of the room.

I laughed. "Right, well, let's move this party outside then. I'm afraid we're filling up seats meant for actual patients."

The women turned, beginning to file quietly out of the room.

"How did you do that?" Kat hissed, elbowing me in the side.

I pretended not to notice. "Do what?"

"Control them like that?"

I shrugged. "Animal magnetism?"

She rolled her eyes, a small smile playing at the corners of her mouth. "Bollocks. You're far too charming for your own good. You know that, right?"

I leaned in, aware of the fact some of the women were watching us suspiciously. "Absolutely."

And, never one to miss an opportunity, I closed the gap between us and kissed her.

CHAPTER 7

My body stiffened as Hayden's mouth covered mine, his body brushing mine as he stepped closer.

For a moment I rejected his advance, determined to maintain my initial impression that this man was nothing but a cad. A player. An arrogant Astipian with far too much charm.

Then his lips moved, and I noticed how soft but firm they were. They were far too soft and much too generous for such an overtly masculine individual like Hayden Dogg.

Then his arms wrapped around me, his body pressing insistently against mine as sparks of delicious awareness tingled up and down my body, rippling out from every contact point.

Well, really. How is any woman to resist such an onslaught to her senses?

I gave in to his kiss, my lips opening under his, my body pressing closer as I tried to make sense of this attraction.

It's not as if I like him. He's far too—

All thoughts evaporated as his tongue dipped into my mouth, teasing my own. With an approving sound, I allowed him greater access, pressing myself into him, plastering us together.

This new position had me pressing against something rather large in Doctor Dogg's pants.

Oh, good, Lord. That can't be what I think it is. It's far too large for it to be... well, that!

Either way, my body reacted, a warm heat pooling deep in my abdomen, anticipation setting my blood on fire.

"Ah-hem." Someone coughed behind me.

We ignored them, Hayden's hand coming up to cup my face, his fingers tangling in the strands of hair that had fallen loose from my ponytail.

He really is the most delightful kisser.

"Excuse me?" the voice said again, this time reaching out to tap on my shoulder. "Sorry to interrupt but we were hoping for an interview?"

I broke the kiss, reality smacking me in the face.

Hoard of women. Arrogant Astipian. NO KISSING!

I stepped back, flushed and far too aroused to be of much use to anyone for the next half hour.

"Right, interview. He's all yours," I told the reporter. Without a backward glance at Hayden, I beat a quick retreat, heading for the staff room doors.

"Kat, wait!"

"Her name is Kat? As in Kat and Dogg? That's perfect! Harold, did you get any footage of that kiss? Should we get Ms. Kat back here to—"

Whatever the reporter had been about to say was cut off as the door slapped closed behind me, shutting out the noise of reception and blocking me from Hayden.

Silly girl! I chastised myself silently as I rushed through the clinic, snatching up my camera gear and heading out to the shelter. *You know better than to tangle with a man as good-looking as Hayden. Remember what happened last time?*

My body, traitor that she was, didn't appear

to care about the potential heartache that lay in the form of Hayden Dogg. It ached, desire continuing to sizzle in my blood long after the kiss.

I buried myself in my work, determined to get this job completed before I did something stupid—like fall in love.

CHAPTER 8

Hayden

I t took me far longer than I expected to
extricate myself from the throng of
admirers. Luckily for me, the heterosexual
single men of this town were more efficient
than bloodhounds when it came to single
ladies, and before I could crush any dreams, the
women were being swept into coffee dates and
charmed into long walks along the beach.

Thank the gods for that.

I loved Capricorn Cove, but this town was
full of crazy people determined to drive me up
the wall—and that included one sassy brunette
with a camera.

I leaned against the door jam, crossing my

arms and legs as I watched, with some amusement, my dog charm Kat.

"Alright, little man," Kat cooed to Hendrix. "You keep giving me that great smile and I'll keep feeding you these yummy treats."

Hendrix's tail whipped back and forth faster than my gaze could catch. He lifted one paw, attempting to bat at the toy she held above his head in one hand, snapping pictures on the camera set on the tripod with her other.

"Good boy!" she praised, adjusting herself and the camera slightly. "What a good boy."

I'd always known I was a pervert. My cock's reaction to her praise for my dog confirmed it. My body wanted her, badly.

Fuck.

"I know you're there. Stop being a creeper and come help me."

I barked out a laugh, pushing away from the jamb and crossing the yard to settle in beside my little pupper.

"Hey buddy," I greeted as he leapt from the basket into my lap, his body wiggling all over mine as he tried to lick my face. "Settle, Hendrix. Let's try that sitting thing we did last night. Ready? Sit!"

The puppy's butt dropped to the ground, his tail sending his rear wiggling.

"Good boy!" I pulled a treat from my

pocket, feeding him the snack. "What a clever little boy you are."

Kat snapped a picture, pulling back from the camera with a grin. "I'll send you that shot free of charge. It was too cute to miss." She reached out, smoothing a hand down Hendrix's back. "And they only stay this little for a short period. You want all the photos you can get."

That gave me an idea.

"You're right. Look, not sure if you'd be interested but Hendrix and I are planning on going hiking tomorrow over to the rock pools. Would you like to join us?"

She considered me for a moment.

"And your brother as well, of course."

Hendrix, turning out to be the best wingman I could have asked for, tumbled out of my lap and flopped at Kat's feet, immediately attacking the lace on her sneakers.

She bent down, ruffling his ears and grinning as he dropped the lace, lapping at her fingers.

"Okay, we could do that, I guess."

Despite her bland words, her eyes twinkled, a pleasant flush colouring her cheeks.

Oh, she's into you. Or just likes your dog. Either way, more opportunities to win her over.

"Great, I'll pick you up at six."

"Six. As in, in the morning?"

I laughed. "Fine, would nine be better?"

"Only if you're bringing coffee and pastries."

"Done."

I held out my hand for her to shake. As she laid her palm against mine, my skin tingled with awareness.

We need all the chances we can get.

"Just so you know, I still really dislike you," Kat said, giving my hand an extra hard squeeze.

I leaned in. "Tell that to your lips."

Before she could fire back at me, or cancel our agreed excursion, I dropped her hand, pushing to a stand and quickly walking away, pleased to hear her muttered outrage carrying on the breeze.

CHAPTER 9

Kat

I sipped the coffee Hayden had handed me, watching as my brother, Hendrix, and Hayden scrambled over rocks and peered into rock pools, trading insults, jabs, and teasing as the two men and dog had the time of their life.

Of course, my brother likes him.

Hayden was exactly the kind of guy my brother would be friends with. They were two peas in a pod, passionate, charming, and overly friendly. People liked them.

People tolerated me.

I looked back down at my coffee cup, absently swirling the remaining liquid as I opened my emotional dungeon, allowing myself to examine memories I'd been determined to banish.

"Kat! I'm just going to check out the bookstore. Are you good here?" Henry called from the edge of one of the rock pools.

"Go! I know you've been dying to commune with the written word since we arrived. Go forth with my blessing." I waved him off, grinning as he punched the air with his fist then took off at a run.

"He's an interesting character, your brother." Hayden flopped down beside me, brushing hair off his forehead.

"Interesting how?"

He shrugged. "Just interesting. Lots of cool facts and figures. Quotes famous people like it's no big deal. I like him."

I grinned. "I like him too. Most of the time."

"I feel that."

Hendrix dropped a twig at Hayden's feet, growling playfully for him to throw it.

"Sit."

When the puppy sat, Hayden tossed it a little way, smiling when the puppy chased it.

"Do you have siblings as well?" I asked, intrigued by his comment.

"Yeah, six now. I'm the eldest. My parents broke up soon after I was born. I was a teenage mistake, but hey, I got cool parents out of it."

"Do they still live here?"

"Dad does. Mom moved south a few years back, and I followed for college. I did part of my residency there but missed the Cove."

"When did you buy the clinic?"

"Two years ago. Mortgaged myself to the hilt, but it's been worth it. We overhauled everything, but it's mine, you know? Something to put my stamp on and say, 'I'm proud of this.'"

I lifted my camera. "I get that. It's how I feel every time I see my photographs somewhere unexpected. I get this little thrill of excitement."

"Exactly."

We grinned at each other for a moment then I broke eye contact, looking towards Hendrix.

"You said six siblings? Did your mom or dad remarry?"

"Neither. Mom's a bit of a lone wolf so has stayed single and ready to mingle, but is also super happy to be alone. Dad's a pack animal. He adopted Jay, James, Ash, Ryan, and Sam. The boys are all younger than me—ranging in age from twenty-six to nine. Then Dad found the love of his life last year, and they just had a baby girl, Janeane."

He shifted forward as he tossed Hendrix's stick again, pulling his phone from his pocket.

"This is Janie-bubba." His lock screen was a picture of him cuddling the tiniest newborn I'd ever seen.

"Oh my goodness," I breathed, my ovaries exploding at her blissed-out little expression. "She's adorable."

"A more than welcome addition to the Dogg Pack," Hayden agreed.

His phone buzzed, a text appearing on the screen.

JAY

So did you ask out the hot photographer? Or did you pussy out like you normally do?

"Fuck!" Hayden swiped up, dismissing the text. "Shit, sorry. Fuck. That's Jay. Ignore him. He's a bastard. Gives us all a bad name. Worst brother ever. Fuck."

An unidentified emotion took root in my chest, its warm tendrils slowly unfurling like new petals, opening me up to a previously unobtainable thought.

Gavin never told anyone about us.

"I broke up with my boyfriend six months ago." The words stopped Hayden's apology.

"Uh... I'm sorry?"

"I'm not." I shrugged. "My parents thought he hung the moon. My friends adored him. He wowed everyone he met—well, except Henry. He hated him."

Hayden nodded, his gaze sharp as he watched me.

"Gavin's charm is why I ignored the red flags. We'd been dating for nine months, but he'd never once taken me to bed. Beyond the occasional make-out session, I just assumed he was being respectful and looking out for me. He was my agent, you see. Said I had the talent to become the next Annie Leibovitz or Robert Frank if I so wished." I glanced his way. "And you have to understand, Hayden, I did. I wanted it so badly. Ever since I first picked up a camera, I've wanted this to be my career, my life."

He nodded, his hand reaching out to capture mine. "I get it. And just so you know, I appreciate you telling me this, but if it makes you uncomfortable, you don't have to."

I sucked in a breath, shaking my head. "No, it's good to get it out."

I looked back at the sea, determined to purge my soul of the embarrassment and hurt that had tainted the last six months of my life.

"Gavin promised me the world, and he delivered. He set up my first and second shows —all of which resulted in sell-outs. It's practically unheard of. I was approached by

British Vogue to shoot their spring-summer edition, it was a dream come true. And all thanks to my boyfriend."

I closed my eyes, my cheeks beginning to burn. "I thought he was going to propose. Instead, I found him with his secretary. His *male* secretary. It wasn't that he's gay that hurt, I'm glad he's finally living his truth. It's that he used me. He knew all along I wasn't the one who could make him happy, and yet he continued to act as if I were his world. I later found out the reason he didn't introduce me to his friends or family was because they all knew about their relationship. I was going to be the work-wife, the one he could trot out for functions and show off to potential clients."

Hayden squeezed my hand, offering comfort but allowing me space to get this off my chest.

"He was also attractive. It's why I'm biased against you."

Hayden grinned, but it didn't quite meet his eyes. "We're not all dicks."

"I know. It's just...." I didn't know how to describe what I was thinking or feeling. "I don't trust my attraction to you."

Hayden rocked back, his expression thoughtful. "What if it doesn't have to be as hard as you're making it?"

"What do you mean?"

"What if we just take this slow and start as friends?"

I raised an eyebrow. "I'm sorry, friends?"

He grinned. "Fine, less than enemies then."

Laughter bubbled up my throat. "Less than enemies it is."

"Accepted acquaintances," Hayden agreed, reaching out a hand to help me up.

"Collegial connections." I allowed him to pull me to a stand.

"Associates that kiss."

"Wait," I sputtered as his hands came up to frame my face. "What!"

His lips captured mine, and once again, I found myself tumbling into a pit of needy, delicious attraction.

CHAPTER 10

Kat tasted of fire and brimstone and bad choices. I knew I'd regret this kiss the moment it was done—but I couldn't help it. Her admission that she was attracted to me but unable to trust it had set me off.

Trust this. Trust me. Trust us. We're so good together, Kitty-Kat.

I began to pull back but her arms came up, wrapping around my neck to press me close to her. A soft protestation slipping free.

Oh, yes.

Kat, I was fast learning, required me to kiss her often. When we kissed, she forgot to doubt.

She forgot that she didn't trust herself and simply gave into the connection between us.

I got you. I won't let you fall.

The connection between us was undeniable. I might not have recognised it the first time I'd seen her, crouched over Gus, that pinched, worried expression on her face. But I certainly hadn't missed it the second time we'd met.

Kat Tenil was my match. She was my swan. My lovebird, my European Beaver.

She was my mate. For life.

This might have started as puppy love, but I knew that I'd move heaven and earth to love her.

Now I just needed to convince her of that fact.

She pulled back, her eyes glassy with desire, her lips wet and red and deliciously puffy.

"This doesn't mean I like you."

"Keep telling yourself that, Kitty-Kat." I kissed her again, this time deeper, our bodies warring for control.

I let her win, allowing her to dominate the kiss, allowing her to own it. Revelling in her power and her utter delight.

"Don't," she panted between kisses, "get comfortable. This is a one-time thing."

"Mm, sure." I cupped her ass. "You want my body real bad."

"No more than you want mine."

I groaned, burying my head in her neck—aware of the fact we were engaging in a rather hot and heavy display of affection on what was a public and very family-friendly beach.

Cool it down, Hayden. You gotta woo the girl.

"As much as I want to continue this," I told her regretfully. "We should go find your brother and get this little guy home."

Hendrix looked up from where he'd been chewing the stick sleepily beside us.

Kat attempted to step back, her face shuttering all expression.

"But," I said, holding her tight to me. "We should definitely do dinner tonight. And maybe tomorrow. Scratch that, tell June I'm coming over every night this week."

Her shell cracked a little spark of hope slipping through. "Really? You'd brave June's cooking for me?"

"No. I'll tell Don to cook."

She slapped my chest, laughter spilling freely between us. "You beast!"

I grinned. "Is that a yes? Can I monopolise your evenings?"

Kat tilted her head to one side, her lips pressing together for a long moment.

"Alright. But only if you bring dessert."

"That," I promised. "I can do."

CHAPTER 11

Kat

True to his word, Hayden turned up slightly before 7 pm. He wore beige chinos and a purple dress shirt with the sleeves rolled back to his biceps. My body actually quivered when I saw him.

*What was it about a guy with his sleeves rolled back? It feels like Victorian-Era porn and yet.... *purrs**

Added to that, the man had brought dessert and a puppy.

This man is dangerous with a capital D.

The naughty side of me looked forward to experiencing that D up close and personal.

"I wasn't sure what you were into," Hayden explained as he handed over two lots of dessert.

"I played it safe and went key lime pie and cupcakes. Everyone loves a cupcake, right?"

I tried not to grin as I accepted the offered treats. "Didn't I mention I'm on a sugar cleanse?"

He froze. "Shit. No. Damn. Wait, there's a place in town that does sugar-free treats. Let me just—"

I burst out laughing, that warm tingling feeling washing over me at the genuine panic in his voice. "I'm kidding, Hayden. Go grab a beer and sit on the deck. Don is barbecuing something that smells wonderful."

I popped the desserts in the fridge and then followed him out, finding him and Henry already bonding. It felt weird that my brother liked him. His relationship with Gavin had been fraught at best and downright hostile at worst. I'd never understood it, and Henry had never been able to articulate his feelings beyond a general sense of distrust.

And hadn't he been correct?

That warm feeling began to dissipate, uncertainty and doubt replacing it.

What if this is another Gavin scenario? What if I'm just a summer-time fling? I'm not sure I can go through that again.

I took the seat next to Hayden, determined to at least give him the benefit of the doubt for one night. I could make my mind up about him after tonight.

"I go out with a few of the guys in town regularly," Hayden was saying to Henry as I sat down. "You guys should come. A few of them have new girlfriends, it's turning into a couples outing now."

Gavin never invited you to meet his friends.

Henry glanced my way, and I could see my thoughts reflected in his expression.

"And your family? How often do you see them?"

I sipped my beer, trying not to grin at Henry's casual tone as he skilfully grilled Hayden, attempting to dig up all the dirt.

"Not as often as I'd like in person with my shift hours. But we video-chat at least once or twice a week. And the group text chat is a constant stream of updates. I miss them like crazy if it's been a few weeks between seeing them but sometimes, seeing the crap they post, I'm glad to have a little distance between us."

Henry's lips pressed into a thin line at that pronouncement, but Hayden didn't see, he was still chuckling as he pulled out his phone to toss to my brother.

"That's my youngest sibling. Janeane had a slight poo explosion. I've never been more grateful to have left home."

I looked over Henry's shoulder, gagging slightly at the photo.

"Oh dear," Henry chuckled, handing the phone back. "Was she ill?"

"Picked up a gastro bug from Sam, my youngest brother. They're both fine now, but it was a gnarly few days for Dad and Karen."

June plunked a large bowl of salad down on the table, Don following with a steaming tray of deliciously seasoned and perfectly grilled chicken.

"Here we go, kids. Dig in."

Food was served as we chatted about work, swapping stories. Henry had spent his day in the bookstore, having discovered they had a rare book collection.

"And you, Kat?" June asked, scooping up another spoonful of the delicious grain salad she's created. "How was your day?"

"Well, I finished all the edits for the calendar. You guys should be good to place an order next week once you decide which photos to use."

"Holy sh—er, shoot." Hayden corrected, glancing at Don. "That's awesome. Thanks for smashing it out, Kat. We all appreciate it."

I waved off his thanks. "No worries. It's all a tax write-off for me if I can say it's for charity."

I said it dismissively, but I'd loved doing it. Capturing an animal wasn't the same as a human. Animals didn't perform how you wanted them to, and capturing their individual personality was harder than it looked.

And the shoot had birthed a second idea that was slowly starting to take shape.

"What will you do with your time now?" Don asked, leaning back in his chair and sipping his cider.

"I'm planning to explore the town and see what sparks my interest."

"Ah, to be young and a starving artist," June moaned wistfully. "I miss the days of free-spirited travel, going wherever the wind—or band—took me."

I chuckled, feeling Hayden's leg pressing against mine.

"My darling, you took off to Ghana last year with only a week's notice. Your days of travel aren't behind you just yet."

June fluttered a hand Don's way. "There's a difference between a lark and the traveller's way of life. I'm afraid you've domesticated me, Donald."

He chuckled, leaning over to kiss her cheek. "I could never change you."

My heart sighed as I watched them nuzzle

into each other, wishing that I could have everything they had found.

Hayden's phone chirped, the ring tone to Baha Men's 'Who let the dogs out.'

I giggled, amused as his cheeks flushed.

"Sorry, this is Sam. I'll just be a second."

He stood up, walking to the edge of the deck and raised the phone to activate the video call.

"Hey, Sammy, what's up, bud?"

"I want to come live with you. Dad won't let me get a dog. He said I had to wait until Janeane is older."

Hayden pinched the bridge of his nose. "Buddy, you know I love you, but you need to stay at home. Karen and Dad are right, a puppy is a big responsibility and probably not one you should get until Janie is a little older."

"But—"

"Sammy, who are you on the phone to?"

Hayden glanced over, finding me watching him. He made a face, rolling his eyes as Sam called, "No one!"

"Is that Hayden? Hayden! How are you? How's it going with the hot photographer?"

Hayden sighed, beginning to walk back to the table.

"Hey, Karrie. It's going well, I think. Let me

introduce you to her family with whom I am trying to have dinner."

By this stage, Henry had lost it; he'd doubled over, his shoulders shaking with silent hilarity while Don and June leaned into each other, smiles wide and approving.

"You know," I commented lightly as he settled in beside me. "That's the second time I've been referred to by your family as the 'hot photographer.'"

"Well, he failed to tell us your name!" The woman on the screen called, waving vigorously. "Hey, I'm Karen, and this is Sam."

She tilted the phone down to show a sullen-looking nine-year-old with a riot of auburn hair.

"Well, hello. I'm Kat."

This had to be the strangest, and sweetest, meet the family I'd ever experienced.

"I don't want a cat. What about my dog?" Sam moaned.

"No, honey. That's her name. Kat. And it's lovely to meet you. I hope Hayden's treating you well."

"Perfectly," I told her, aware of the fact my family was also observing this strange introduction. "And I'm sorry you're not getting a dog, Sam."

"Oh, he is. I just need to convince his father." Karen waved a hand, upsetting the camera on her side. "Will just needs the right incentive."

"We're not getting a dog!" A voice called off screen.

"Of course not, honey!" Karen called, sending a wink to the camera.

"Wait, did I hear you're speaking to the hot photographer? Put her on! I wanna introduce her to the J-Man." A second voice demanded.

Hayden sighed, his eyes drifting closed, his face taking on a pained expression.

"I shouldn't have picked up. I knew I shouldn't have picked up."

He shifted closer, our thighs pressing together as his arm wrapped around my shoulder and he pulled me into his side.

"Family, meet Kat."

Before I knew it, all of Hayden's brothers were on screen, and I was introduced to his father and then dragged into the dog-no-dog debate. An hour later, we finally ended the call, with Henry promising to call Jay with book recommendations in the next day or so.

As Hayden farewelled his family, June leaned in. "This could be your life if you let yourself love Hayden."

I blinked at her, stunned. "June, I'm not here to stay."

"Why not?"

Hayden returned, dropping into the seat beside me. "Sorry about that, they're all a little crazy."

"All good," I told him. "Shall we start dessert?"

Over pie and cupcakes, we talked literature and music, listening to June and Don as they entertained us with stories of life on the road.

Once all the plates were cleared, Hayden caught my hand, entwining our fingers. "Shall we go for a walk along the beach?"

"Yeah, I'd like that."

CHAPTER 12

Hayden

I felt a million feet tall as we walked along the sand, Kat's body leaning into mine. As annoying as my family were, I adored them. And their interference had worked in my favour. Whatever barrier Kat had erected between us had more chips in it than a crumbling castle. I still wasn't sure how to win her over completely, but I was more than willing to keep working on it.

She was worth it.

"Did you like the pictures?" She broke the easy silence between us.

"Loved them. The one of Hendrix is going on the mantel at home."

"You have a mantel?"

"Yeah, you wanna see it? My house is only a street over."

She paused, her feet digging into the sand.

For a moment, she seemed stricken, unsure. Then her face cleared, a determined expression taking up residence.

"I'd love to."

We walked the short distance to my house in silence. I'd left a sleeping Hendrix on June's back deck, Henry waving us off with a promise that he'd keep an eye on him.

"Go, have fun. I'll be here enjoying my date with one Ms. Austen." He'd held the book as if it were a lover.

If I had a sister who was older than three months, I'd let him date her.

"This is it," I said to Kat, opening the little gate at the front of the beach shack. "It's not big, but it gets the job done."

I led her up the rambling path, the front porch covered in creeping succulents.

"Couldn't afford much once I bought the clinic. Old Mrs. Rogers was moving in with her daughter and offered me this place for a steal. It's only two-bedroom and what could barely be classified as a bathroom. But it's comfortable and neat and—"

"Hayden."

"Yeah?"

"Just open the door."

"Right, sorry."

I pushed it open, sweeping my arms out. "Welcome to—oof!"

Kat threw herself at me, pressing my back into the door, her mouth finding mine.

"Less talk," she ordered, kissing me over and over as her hands fisted my shirt, attempting to shove it up my body. "More nakedness."

A better man might have attempted to slow this situation down. He might have asked if she was certain this is what she wanted. He might even have asked if she wanted to have a proper alone dinner before he took her to bed.

I was *not* that man.

I couldn't even wait the ten seconds it would take to walk to my bedroom. I wanted her now.

"Kat," I groaned, helping her with my fly. "Please tell me you're getting naked too?"

I wondered if she'd refuse, if this was just some way to get me naked then leave me wanting.

"Soon," she promised, tugging my pants down my thighs. "I just want to see what I'm working with first."

I huffed out a laugh as she stripped me and

then stepped back, her gaze hot and bright with desire.

"Like what you see?" I asked, spreading my arms out.

"Mm, very much." She reached out a hand, wrapping it around my cock.

My eyes crossed, my brain malfunctioning as Kat stroked me, fisting my cock hard as she pressed delicate kisses to my collarbone.

"Kitty-Kat," I groaned, tilting my head back to give her access to my neck. "Are you gonna let me touch you?"

"In a minute."

Her teeth grazed the seam of my neck, her lips pressing to my pulse point as she bit and sucked at my skin, little noises of pleasure escaping from between her lips as she continued to stroke me.

I will not come. I will not come. I will not come.

The words became a rhythmic chant as I tried to ignore the desperate heat pulsing through my body.

Fuckity fucking fuckity fuck!

Unable to stand another second of this sweet torture, my hands lifted, fisting the material of her dress as I tugged it up her body, revealing yards of naked skin.

No panties. No bra. Perfect body made for me. Brain does not compute. Hold for restart.

A sound escaped me. Brutal, raw, desperate.

I dropped to my knees, gently prying her legs open, my tongue seeking her taste.

Kat sighed, her body falling back against the wall as I feasted upon her. As her desire coated my face, I vowed to commit her taste to memory, knowing I'd want to remember this moment until my dying day.

"Hayden," she moaned, her fingers pressing me closer. "Please."

I shifted, pressing one finger inside her, my tongue and lips finding her clit–licking and sucking in equal measure, gaging what pace, what action, what pressure left her gasping.

I glanced up, noting that I had yet to taste her rose-coloured nipples, or her collarbone, or the tender skin behind her earlobe.

Soon. As soon as I make her come, we'll get to those.

I upped my efforts, focusing on driving her mad, desperate to make this the best moment of her life.

Come for me, Kitty-Kat. Let me taste you.

Her body arched, her legs squeezing my head as she cried out, her body clenching around my finger as she came in a lusty, noisy, beautiful mess.

I used my shoulders to brace her, holding Kat up, and pressing gentle kisses against the inside of her thighs as she caught her breath.

If I tried really hard, I could almost ignore the sweet ache of my dick as he begged to be balls-deep in her tight snatch.

"Hayden?"

"Yes, baby?"

Her head lolled back against the wall, her fingers flexing in my hair. "Did you learn that in vet school?"

I grinned. "Nope. That was all me."

"Mm. Well, you got any more tricks, Doctor Dogg?"

I surged to my feet, pressing my body against hers. "Oh, I might have a few up my sleeve."

Kat's eyelids fluttered open, a sated smile on her gorgeous face. "Well, by all means, teach me."

Not sure when I died, but I sure am happy to be in heaven.

I kissed her deeply, letting her taste her cream on my tongue, then dipped my head to her breast, nuzzling and sucking at her areola, pulling moans from her greedy mouth.

"Hayden," she moaned, cupping her breasts and offering them to me. "Baby...."

Fuck this.

I bent, hooking my hands behind her legs and lifting her, pressing her back against the wall until she wrapped her legs and arms around me.

"Hayden, what are you—?"

I staggered down the hall to the bedroom, my erection making it difficult to walk.

"Moving us to a—" I dropped her on the bed, immediately covering her with my body. "—comfier surface."

We kissed, our mouths making fierce love as hands moved overheated skin, bodies hard and hot.

My cock throbbed as Kat reached down, gripping me in one hand and stroking me up and down lazily.

"Like what you feel?" I panted around kisses.

"God, yes." She groaned against my lips, her legs falling open to cradle me. "Condom?"

"Side table."

She reached for the drawer, pulled a strip free and handed them to me. I ripped into the foil, rolling one down my cock, desperate to feel her around me.

"Ready?"

"Get in me, Vet-boy."

With a grin, I moved, positioning us just so. Our mouths danced together, tongues twisting and stroking as we heightened the anticipation.

"Hayden, hurry the fuck—"

I thrust in, cutting Kat's complaint off. We both groaned, the friction almost too much to handle.

Don't you dare come!

"More!" she demanded, her legs wrapping around me. "Harder!"

Well, this settles it. I'm in love.

I gave in to the need to brand myself on her body. I drove hard, fucking viciously into her tight little snatch, loving how she clutched me, loving the tightness of her, the feel of her breasts against my chest, the taste of her on my tongue, the sent of us together as we made love.

I dropped a hand, finding her clit, pressing it in that way she seemed to love. Kat arched back, her pussy milking my cock as she came.

Thank fuck!

"Kat." I thrust twice more, grunting her name and emptying myself into the woman I loved.

Wait. Woman I loved? Love? Wow. You move fast, Dogg.

I collapsed on her, both of us panting,

sweaty messes as we fought the last of the desire singing through our veins.

I rolled off her, enjoying the way she snuggled into my side, her hand resting on my stomach as we both tried to catch our breath.

The realisation I loved Kat sat with me in the best possible way. I loved her. I wanted to spend the rest of my life with her. I wanted to travel with her to places unseen, experiencing the joy of them through her eyes and reminiscing about them in twenty years, thanks to the talent of her camera.

Well, heck. How am I gonna tell her?

"Hayden," she whispered, reaching a hand up to cup my cheek. "That was incredible. Only...."

"Only? I asked, completely blissed out on endorphins.

"Can we do it again? And soon?"

"How soon?" I asked, cocking one eyebrow.

"Like, say, ten minutes?"

We grinned at each other in the dim light.

"Baby, we can do whatever you want."

And we did. Four more times.

CHAPTER 13

Kat

Hayden hadn't lied when he said he wanted to monopolise my evenings. Every night after work, he was at June's dining table sharing jokes with Henry, teasing me, and devouring Don's cooking.

Some nights he took me to local bars or restaurants, feeding me delicious morsels of local specialties or forcing me onto the dance floor, where he proved that white men really couldn't dance.

And I, silly girl that I am, began to fall under his spell. Perhaps it was the mid-summer atmosphere or the way he made me laugh. Perhaps it was the mind-blowing sex that only seemed to get better the longer I spent with him—but every moment seemed to end too soon. I wanted more laughs, more deep conversations, and far more kisses.

My need terrified me. Hayden Dogg was the kind of man a woman fell in love with. He was the kind of guy that you didn't get over. He'd always be the one that got away.

I was only meant to be in town for the summer, then it was off to travel around the islands, documenting my journey through the lens of a camera.

Love had never factored into my plan. Now I was considering all sorts of crazy things—like abandoning my plan and remaining in the Cove instead.

Time to get to work, Kat. You can think about the good Doctor later.

Try as I might, I found myself daydreaming of him as I spent my days photographing the remnants of the early years of the town and interviewing some of the elders. A vague idea of what my next show may feature had begun to take root. Far too early to explain, I simply went where my gut told me.

Which is how I found myself standing on the edge of the old pier, seagulls circling above me as waves gently crashed into the slowly rotting wood, snapping pictures even though my mind was on one rather sexy vet across town.

As if I had the power to summon him, my cell vibrated in my pocket. I pulled it free, grinning when I saw Hayden's name.

"Well, hello Doctor Dogg, to what do I owe this pleasure?"

"Hey Kitty-Kat, I just needed to hear your voice."

I straightened, focusing in on him, not liking the note of sadness I detected in his tone.

"Are you alright?"

He sighed heavily. "We lost a patient. I'd been hoping he'd pull through, but it wasn't to be. The owners are understandably devastated, and I fucking hate losing any of my patients. It's the worst part of my job."

"I'm sorry. What can I do?"

"You're doing it. I just needed to hear your voice. I needed something positive to focus on for ten minutes."

"Positive or distracting?"

He chuckled. "Positive."

"I'll distract you anyway. I'm not wearing matching underwear. Wanna know why?"

Hayden sucked in a breath. "Kat...."

"Because I'm not wearing a bra. Fuck those contraptions."

Hayden's voice sounded strained for a

different reason. "Baby, you know I love this witty banter we have going on, but this is too far. A man can't resist this kind of temptation."

I grinned. "Are you having a better day now?"

"Mm, thank you."

"Any time."

"I should get back to it." I could hear the reluctance in his tone.

"How about I cook dinner tonight?"

"Are you a better cook than June?"

I laughed. "Much better. I'll see you at ho— I mean, your house."

He let my faux pas slide.

"Okay, see you soon, Kitty-Kat."

I hung up, my gaze drawn to the seagulls as they swooped in the breeze.

Home.

I pushed the thought away for the moment, determined to examine it in the future when I didn't have a boyfriend who was hurting.

Perhaps I can't take away his heartache, but I can make him feel better.

The door pushed open, and I heard Hendrix run to greet Hayden.

"Hey buddy, is your momma home? Kat, are you here?"

I grinned, settling back on the bed. "In the bedroom. Can you give Hendrix his toy and then come here? I need a hand."

I heard Hayden drop his keys on the entry table, then the solid thud of Hendrix's toy as he dropped it on the ground.

"There you go, buddy, that should keep you busy for ten minutes."

I closed my eyes, relishing the anticipation as he walked down the hall, listening to his heavy steps as they fell against the wood flooring.

I'd left the bedroom door slightly ajar. I opened my eyes, watching as he pushed it open.

"Hey, baby," I said with a welcoming smile. "Can you help me with this?"

The vibrator purred deliciously against my clit as Hayden stood staring in the doorway. I was completely naked but for a crotchless lace teddy that left nothing to the imagination.

I knew he could see how wet I was from across the room, and I watched as he swallowed, gratified to see his reaction.

"Did I die and go to heaven?"

With a wicked grin, I spread my legs wider, pressing the vibrator more firmly to my clit, groaning at the sensation, my head falling back to the pillow.

"Aren't you going to help me?" I asked in a little pouty voice. "I'm so empty, Doctor."

Hayden moved, kicking the door shut behind him as he began to strip, tripping over his own feet in his rush to the bed.

Come closer, said the spider to the fly.

By the time he hit the bed, he was naked but for his socks.

Oh, but he is adorable.

"You like?" I asked, running one hand up my body to cup a lace-covered breast.

Hayden's answer was to wrap his hands around my ankles and yank me down the bed.

I squealed, losing my grip on the vibrator.

"You don't need it," he barked, climbing up onto the bed, his cock thick and heavy and ready to fuck me raw.

"Hayden!"

His head dropped, his lips closing around one nipple as his fingers slid through my slick heat, his groan so deeply guttural and approving that my body clenched in response.

"Someone," he whispered as he transferred his mouth from one nipple to the other. "Has been a very naughty girl."

"Never," I protested, closing my eyes against the onslaught of feelings his touch inspired. "I'm only ever your good girl."

Hayden fisted his cock, running it through my wet lips until he found my clit. He used the tip as a weapon, determined to conquer me through filthy play.

"You are driving me fucking crazy, Kat. I need to be in you."

I shuddered. "Yes, Doctor."

Instead of allowing him to press me back into the mattress, I rose. My lips found his cock and wrapped urgently around it. I wanted to taste the salt on his skin, to catch the precum with my tongue.

I fisted the base of his cock, pressing forward to take him deeper into my mouth.

"Fuck!" Hayden barked, tangling his fingers in my hair. "Fuck!"

I stroked his length with my tongue, flicking playfully at the underside of cock, enjoying the litany of curses Hayden muttered as I teased him.

"Fuck. Fuck. God damn it. Fuck!"

"Take it, you filthy girl. Suck me harder, Kat. You want my cum, you take it. Fuck that big cock."

My body pulsed with need, begging me to stop and fill myself up with him. Instead, I focused on Hayden's pleasure, determined to make this last.

But Hayden—it seemed—had other ideas.

He reared back, pulling his cock from my mouth and reaching for me. He flipped me over, pressing my front into the bed as he lined up his cock behind me.

"Hayden!" I screamed as he thrust into me, his chest pressing against my back. "Hayden!"

At once, everything was too much and not enough. He felt huge in me, too heavy on top of me. And yet I relished his weight. I loved the way my body had to stretch to accommodate his cock, the sweet burn as he fucked me with little regard for pace or pleasure. So completely mindless in his own desperation that I was nothing but a vessel for his cum.

"That's it!" I cried as my orgasm hovered. "Fuck me, Hayden! Take me!"

He thrust deep, pulling out to thrust once again. I cried out as his hand gripped my hair, tugging my head back, giving him access to my neck.

"Come!" he demanded, teeth nipping at my throat. "Come for me!"

I broke, my body milking his cock, spasming around him as we both came—wet, loud, and fucking perfect.

In the aftermath, we collapsed on the bed, both of us ruined beyond measure.

For a long moment, we lay silent, our breaths the only sound.

I love this man.

The realisation hit me like a bolt of lightning, setting me alight.

I love Hayden Dogg. I want little puppies. I want little people. I want a life with this beautiful man.

I closed my eyes, relishing this feeling of utter perfection. Revelling in the knowledge that I wasn't broken. Whatever I'd felt for Gavin hadn't been anything like this robust, fulsome love. It was laughable how much time and effort I'd wasted on grieving for a relationship that didn't feel even one-tenth as real as this moment.

What about your work? Your career? Your family? You're British. He's Astipian. This can't possibly work.

I thought of June, knowing exactly what she'd say.

Love is love, my darling. And you should always follow your heart. It knows best.

Hayden rolled to his side, staring at me for a long moment.

"You okay?" I asked softly.

"No."

I sat up. "What's—"

"Fuck Kat, I know it's early, but—" He shook his head. "I can't imagine a life without you. And, well, here's the thing. I'm not asking you to marry me just yet. However, I can definitely see that as a possibility. It's just. Well. I want you. I want to follow you wherever you go. So maybe we could try this relationship thing out. Together. I could take a leave from the clinic. We could travel and get your photos. I can take temp jobs—people always need vets. And, well, be together. Experience life together."

This precious man sucked in a breath, his face so desperately earnest that my heart ached for him.

"I love you, Kat."

My aching heart exploded. Warm, honeyed sunshine exploded out of me to bathe everyone and everything within three hundred million miles of this bedroom.

He loves me. He really loves me.

I reached out, cupping his cheek.

"So, here's the thing, Hayden. I'd never ask you to leave your clinic."

He opened his mouth, but I cut him off with a shake of my head.

"No, let me finish. I'd never ask you to because I know the value you give to this community and to that place. It's yours. It's your mark, and you're making a difference."

It was my turn to suck in a breath.

"But here's the thing. I've never had a place to call home. Never wanted one, if I'm honest. But now I know home isn't a place. It's a person. And that person is you."

I leaned in, pressing a quick, chaste kiss to his lips.

"You're my other half, Hayden. So here's the plan. We're going to stay in the Cove. We're going to live in this little house until we can afford a bigger place. We're going to get married on June and Don's deck and force my mother to fly here even though she's never been more than a hundred kilometres from home. We're going to make love under the stars and have an epic honeymoon travelling around Astipia and visiting every inch of coastline and national park. Then we're going to come back here, settle down, and learn how to love through to our happily ever after."

I raised an eyebrow. "Sound good?"

He flipped me over, pressing me back into the mattress.

"Kitty-Kat, that sounds like forever."

"So that's a yes to my marriage proposal, then?"

"That's a fuck yes!"

And he sealed it with a kiss.

EPILOGUE

Kat

London

Twelve months later

"It's the rock pools."
I grinned at my fiancé. "I told you this series is about the Cove."
"I know, it's just... you make the town look way better than it actually is."
I hip-checked Hayden, rolling my eyes. "Don't you dare talk down to our town. Capricorn Cove is the best."
He ignored me, leading us to the next photo in the gallery. It featured June and Don

laughing on their back deck as the sun began to set behind them. I'd caught the years on their faces and the laughter in their eyes as they stared at each other, love written in every part of their being.

I'd entitled this one, *Forever*.

"I know I said this last year at the gallery showing for 'Animalistic' but this love series is freaking amazing."

I grinned, leaning into my husband-to-be, relishing his praise. "Thank you, darling."

For the past year, I'd documented all types of love as I experienced it around me and through my relationship with Hayden. I'd captured mothers giving birth, and children saying goodbye to parents. I'd captured couples and marriages, cancer diagnoses and joyous recoveries, big moments and small.

And you're about to capture the final one.

We walked through the exhibit to a small area I'd specifically designed at the back of the gallery. A TV screen sat on one wall, an X-marked spot in the middle of the small cubicle.

"What's this one?" Hayden asked.

Nervous butterflies took flight in my belly.

"I wanted people to capture their own love. It's a kissing booth—or, more precisely, a love declaration booth."

I pointed to the small button on the side of

the cubicle. "You hit that and it records you for three minutes. It'll send you the message via email, but you become a part of the exhibit."

Hayden grinned. "I love this idea. Let's do it."

He pulled me into his side, turning towards the camera. "Ready?"

I nodded, pressing the button.

The TV flashed—*Recording in Three... Two... One.*

The screen beeped, and a little red light flashed on.

"I love you," Hayden told me. "I can't wait for you to be my wife. I look forward to our wedding day, but more than that one moment, I look forward to our marriage and our life together. Today, tomorrow and forever, I will love you."

I melted against him. "I love you, Hayden Dogg. I love our life together, and I love that we will experience life together. I can't wait for our wedding, even though I'm never going to take your name."

He grinned, knowing he'd well and truly lost the fight for me to become Mrs. Kat Dogg.

I sucked in a breath. "And I can't wait for our baby to arrive." I reached for his hand, pressing it to my stomach. "Congratulations, Daddy."

I'd watch this footage over and over again in the years after. I'd watch his stunned expression then the joy that settled on his features. I'd watch how he dropped to his knees and wrapped his arms around me, pressing his face to my belly. I'd watch how he'd kiss my stomach, then lift his head to meet my gaze.

"I love you, Kitty-Kat. And I love our baby."

That image of him on his knees holding me would always be the best photo I'd ever taken.

Next up in the Dogg Series are Henry and a wallflower that he adores...

Want more Hayden and Kat? Check out the bonus slice of life on my website. www.EvieMitchell.com

*If you enter the code **EBOOK10** you can get 10% off your purchase from my website.*

Be sure to also sign up for my newsletter or check out my website for more book news.

ABOUT THE AUTHOR

Evie Mitchell is a thirty-something romance author (she/her/hers) living with disability. She believes in inclusion, accessibility, and fierce romance. Her loves include steamy romance novels, her husband, their sausage dogs (heaven help her), and her ever-growing collection of book-related mugs.

As a woman with a diverse work history including in areas such as emergency response, event management, human rights, disability access, and security - her books are filled with true stories (bridezillas), worst-case scenarios (malfunctioning dresses), and her favorite tropes (one-bed).

Evie specialises in fiercely inclusive happily ever afters.

ALSO BY EVIE MITCHELL

All Access Series

Knot My Type

Love Flushed

Darn Knit All

Larsson Siblings

Thunder Thighs

Clean Sweep

The X-List

Reality Check

The Christmas Contract

The A-List

Capricorn Cove

The Shake-up

Double the D

Muffin Top

The Mrs. Clause

New Year, Knew You

Double Breasted

As You Wish
You Sleigh Me
Meat Load
Resolution Revolution

Dogg Pack

Bad English
The Frock Up
Pier Pressure
Trick or Trent
New Year's Faye

Reigning Hearts

The Marriage Claim
Silent Knight

Men of Trinity Bay

Kink in the Road

Nameless Souls MC

Runner
Wrath
Ghost
Shield

Elliot Security

Rough Edge
Bleeding Edge